Cold Read

Sharyn Kopf

LoJo Publishing
2014

First Printing: 2014
Second Printing: 2018

ISBN: 978-0692340769

LoJo Publishing
803 E. Sandusky Ave.
Bellefontaine, OH 43311
www.sharynkopf.wordpress.com
www.girlsnightin40.com

Special discounts are available on quantity purchases by corporations, associations, educators, and others. For details, contact the publisher at the above listed address.

U.S. trade bookstores and wholesalers: Please contact LoJo Publishing, tel: (937) 407-7943 or email sharynkopf@gmail.com.

To my sister, Susie Kopf Jarvis, who gave this single woman a sense of family by letting me be a part of hers.

For those unfamiliar with the language, this book contains a glossary of theatre terms on the last page.

Chapter 1
Stephie

*... because it is not always that the hopes of deserving, loving
human beings are blessed ...*
~N. Richard Nash, "The Rainmaker"

It is, quite possibly, the first time I've ever
seen anyone mosey, other than John Wayne. So,
the first time in real life. But mosey he does, right
through the double doors of the Holland Theatre
and straight into my heart, dragging a chill rush of
autumn air in his wake. All six-foot-four of him,
with his bald head and smirky swagger.

Please God. Please let him be here for the auditions.

Auditions always make me nervous, whether
I'm posturing for a part onstage or casting from
the seats below. This time it's the latter—my first
directing job at the old, historic theatre in
downtown Bellefontaine, Ohio. We had just
started auditions, and I was already swiping sweat
from my forehead at the lack of men showing up.
Leave it to me to choose a play that requires six of
them. Everyone knows you have to beg, borrow,
and steal to get more than a handful of guys to
audition for community theatre. So far, eleven
women have read for the one female part
compared to three men for the six male roles. And

of those three, two were teens and the third is perfect for H.C., the main character's dad.

Which means I still haven't found my over-the-top leading man, Starbuck.

And now, here he is, standing in front of me, grinning and handing me his slightly wrinkled audition form. How it got wrinkled from the lobby to here, I ... well, maybe he's nervous too. I stick out my hand. "I'm the director, Stephie Graham, and this is my assistant, Merle Borscht."

He takes my fingers in a firm grip. "Andy Tremont. Is this a cold read?"

"Yes." And if that isn't confirmation enough, I nod so hard my blue-green beret tips forward, knocking lavender-highlighted bangs into my eyes. I brush my vision clear.

"But if you have something ready," I say, "we'd love to see it."

"Uh, nope." He scuffs a shoe on the floor and looks toward the door he just walked through. "I just found out about this today, so I'm not too prepared."

"Oh, that's okay!" I say, tossing out a hand breezily and accidentally smacking Merle in the chest. Which jolts the elderly man out of his reverie long enough to say,

"You have any experience, son?"

Good old Merle. He shuffles everywhere and has thick, white hair and warm eyes and doesn't think anything interesting has happened since the

Rat Pack broke up. I mentioned once I felt the same way about the Brat Pack and he looked at me with such disappointment, I imagine he went home that night and wept for my generation.

But he knows theatre like Sinatra knew Vegas, so I'm lucky to have him on my team. Such as it is.

Andy hooks a thumb into his belt loop, Duke-style, and says, "Oh, sure." He leans over the table I'm perched at and points to the "previous experience" section of his form. "When I lived in Columbus I did a bunch of stuff. Motel in *Fiddler*, the Stage Manager in *Our Town*, and Porthos in an outdoor production of *The Three Musketeers*. That was fun."

I'll bet.

He stands up and his head seems to brush against the star-studded theatre ceiling. His green eyes light into mine. I take a deep breath and catch a whiff of soap and leather. I almost sigh.

Trouble, thy name is Andy.

I stare. I blink. My, but he is tall.

He clears his throat.

Say something, Stephie, before he moseys out of your life.

I finally exhale and whisper, "You sing?" Because that is the most important information necessary for someone who *isn't* auditioning for a musical. I almost smack myself.

He doesn't seem to mind, though. "I do okay."

"Because we're doing a musical in the spring."
Good grief, Stephie.

"I'll keep that in mind."

"Well," I say, trying to regain control of what I'd momentarily lost sight of, "we, um, don't have any other women here at the moment so would you mind reading for Starbuck with, uh, me?"

"Sure."

I hand him the sides for the scene I want him to read and follow him up the ramp and onto the stage.

And he nails it. I have my Starbuck. He's so perfect, I fight the urge to just play Lizzie myself. My youthful fantasy of falling in love with my co-star during a show calls out to me. But how could I? We have plenty of talent in Bellefontaine and, well, I don't really look the part.

Darn it.

Merle grins and gives me a thumbs-up. As I make my way back down the ramp, something crashes to the floor backstage. Andy jumps.

I laugh. "Don't worry. It's just Juniper."

"Juniper?" Andy glances behind him. "Is she auditioning?"

"Oh no," I say, and waggle my eyebrows at him. "She's our resident ghost."

Merle nods. "Every decent theatre has one."

Now Andy smiles. "I'll have to take your word on that."

And then two more women arrive to audition and the moment is over. I don't see him leave but I have his number.

"Andy's perfect," Merle tells me later. "He even reminds me a bit of Peter Lawford."

"I thought Burt Lancaster played Starbuck in the movie."

Merle frowns and sighs, gaping at me like I'm a high school girl speaking in hashtags.

Shoot. I might have just said something else that will make him weep.

❄ ❄ ❄

Later that night, I let myself into my small, one-bedroom apartment. My cat, Cozy, meets me at the door, purring and weaving around my ankles. I pick her up and carry her to my only seating area, a ragged, but clean, red-plaid couch. It isn't much of an apartment—old, ugly, and it somehow always smells like bacon—but they let me have a cat for a reasonable price so it's home enough for me.

"Home is where the heart is, right, Cozy?" The cat looks at me, meows, and bats a paw at my arm. She jumps down and meows again, teeth bared. I sigh. "Oh, all right."

I follow her into the kitchen and refill her food dish, then grab a bottle of cream soda from the fridge. Taking a seat at the kitchen table, which also serves as my work desk, I open my laptop.

First thing I do is Google search for "Peter Lawford." A Rat-Packer, of course. Tall, handsome but with a full head of hair. So, for the most part, Merle was right. Personally, though, Andy reminds me more of a bald Jeff Goldblum.

All in all, he's a nice combination of wonderfulness and swagger and just the guy I need to play Starbuck.

Couldn't ask for more than that.

After turning on a 50s Pandora station, I open the marketing packet I started yesterday for a Marysville dermatologist and get to work.

I finally crawl into bed around two a.m., which is actually pretty early for me. But I toss around all night, messing up the carefully tucked sheets and dreaming about the tall, bald actor who seems destined to break my heart.

Chapter 2
Juniper

September 1933

Juniper Remington waited in the wings of the Holland Theatre, her nerves twisting from her stomach to her throat. How would she ever be able to sing like this?

Maybe I could turn off a few lights. If no one could see me. . . .

That would never work. Not that it mattered anyway. The one person she wanted to see smiling at her from the audience wasn't there. William was gone, and he wouldn't be back. For all she knew, he was already in New York, meeting important people and forgetting all about silly old spinsters with too much love and not enough money.

The pianist, Frederick, came to wait beside her. She glanced at him, then whispered, "I want to sing 'What'll I Do'."

He didn't turn his gaze from the brother and sister juggling act onstage, but his heavy black mustache twitched in the corners. Perhaps he was trying not to laugh. Or he was about to sneeze. "Why would you want to do that? We've been rehearsing 'Someone to Watch Over Me' for three weeks."

Juniper shrugged. "I've changed my mind."

"Whatever you want." And he shrugged too.

She took a deep breath as the Master of Ceremonies, Mr. Van Meer, strode onto the stage to introduce her. It would be over soon. She could sing "What'll I Do" in less than three minutes, and still put in enough heart and soul to bring every feminine eye in the room to tears. Short and effective suited her mood much better tonight.

And perhaps, with that song, she could put William behind her. Still, she knew it would take all her fortitude to get through the last line:

When I'm alone with only dreams of you, that won't come true.

What'll I do?

Chapter 3
Stephie

We hit the stage full force at our first read-through the following Monday. I had to hunt down actors to play the sheriff and his deputy but Ron Morris and Brad Forrester both owe me for helping them put together successful marketing campaigns for their businesses. Besides, they love acting so it wasn't too hard to convince them.

The part of Deputy File is just as important as Starbuck, at least for what I have in mind, and Brad could bring the right amount of pathos and anger and hope to it. Though not as tall as Andy, he is, in several ways, better looking. Mostly because of his full head of thick, black hair and the laugh lines around his soft brown eyes. The contrasts between Andy and Brad are exactly what I need.

I settled on Willa Barnes as Lizzie. Since she typically grabs the lead in most Holland productions, I hesitated, not wanting to perpetuate the cliquish casting I've seen so often in community theatre. I would love to give someone new a chance, but Willa is the best one for the part. She's petite and vulnerable and, though certainly attractive, we could make her come across as plain—like Lizzie is described in the play—with the right makeup and coloring. But though Lizzie is initially considered unattractive, there needs to be a beauty in her that Starbuck sees first, followed by File and, hopefully, the audience.

Best of all, Willa pulls in a crowd. Everybody loves her.

So, cast in place, we sit in a circle and introduce ourselves. As much as we need to anyway. Andy is the only new guy; everyone else has been a Holland regular for years. Next to Andy, I'm the most recent addition and even I've been involved at the theatre since I moved to Bellefontaine three years ago and snagged a chorus part in *The Music Man*.

When I ask how many are familiar with the play, only Willa and Andy raise their hands.

"Well," I say, "my experience with the show has always been that the audience feels disappointed when Lizzie chooses File over Starbuck. With Starbuck portrayed as her soul mate, how could it be any other way?"

I glance at Willa, the only other woman in our circle, and she smiles and nods. Encouraged, I continue. "I want to change that. I would like to perform this in a way that makes the audience happy when she chooses File."

Glancing around at my talented circle of actors, I grin. "But you know what might be even better? If half of the audience wants her with File, but the other half prefers Starbuck. And they leave the show talking about it, even arguing over who they think she should have ended up with."

Turning to Brad, I say, "This puts a lot on you. Even though you seem to reject her in act two, there has to be something in the way you look at her. We can get a lot of this across in blocking, but it has to be there in your performance too."

Brad bobs his head, and I can tell he's considering his character and how to pull that off. Knowing what a committed actor Brad is, I'm confident he's more than capable of making it happen. And he'll probably surprise me in the process.

Then I turn to Andy. "And all you have to be is charismatic and larger than life, but as fleeting as a hummingbird. Think you can handle that?"

He chuckles. "I'll do my best."

By the end of our first reading, I have chills. *The Rainmaker* has been one of my favorite plays for years and now, finally, I have a chance to bring it to life. To add my own flair. To watch a great cast offer new flavors and nuances and attitudes. And, over time, to see that cast become a family. An eight-week, one-time-only family.

It's not a real family, but you take what you can get.

I hand out rehearsal schedules, and we wrap things up. I barely get out, "See you tomorrow," and Andy is out the door. And it occurs to me he might be married. With kids. Why hadn't I thought of that before? He has to be close to forty, if not over it. Good looking. Tall. Dare I use the word "virile"? Someone must have snatched him up by now. Just because I hadn't noticed a ring. . . .

And, just like that, I'm sad enough to sob into my now-flat cream soda. No, wait. In Ohio they call it "pop." Still trying to get used to that one. I wander around the theatre, putting chairs back and turning off lights. I don't even have Merle shuffling around with me; the school board meets the first Monday of the month and, as the middle school principal, he kind of has to be there.

So it's just me, feeling abandoned and morose and thinking about so many other things that, when I flick off the last stage light, it takes me a second to realize one of the lights is, in fact, still on.

Must have missed it.

I try all of the switches—and there are plenty—yet that one light, stage right, hovering over the grand piano they'll let us move after the upcoming Gershwin tribute concert, doesn't even flicker. It has to be one of the switches on the main breaker. I test them all again, three times in fact, and nothing.

That's when a chill crawls up my spine and trickles through my hair.

I whisper, "Juniper?"

And the light switches off.

I grab my things and race out of the building, grateful for the string of floor security lights that show me the way.

❄ ❄ ❄

By the end of week two, I have all three acts blocked. Everyone knows his—or her—exit and entrance and every move in between has been mapped out. It looks great.

On the downside, Jim Hessington, who plays Lizzie's dad, H.C., can't quite seem to get his lines down and asks for a hint every ten seconds, and our sheriff, Ron, has missed half the rehearsals. But he knows finding a replacement at this time would be near-impossible. All I can do is beg him to commit to the show—for my sake and for the sake of the rest of the cast.

I suppose I should be glad that at least Ron calls to let me know. Most of the time. Still, it's beyond frustrating. I consider siccing Juniper on him, but that freaks me out. Instead, I give myself my director pep talk, focusing on the one truth of theatre I've seen happen again and again: The show will go on and it will all come together in the end. I don't know how. But it just will. It's silly for me to worry that this production might somehow break that cardinal rule.

On the other hand, it might. Because that's my life right now.

Besides, these are small things. I have a Starbuck and Lizzie a Broadway director would kill for. Their chemistry sends steam off the stage, and I can't take my eyes off of them. Okay, I can't keep my eyes off of him. Andy brings an enthusiastic, almost boyish, sexiness to his character.

Willa, of course, plays her part with polished professionalism. Which is great, except ... it's almost too polished. I want her to relax and even mess up. Lizzie is a lonely woman, destined for a life of spinsterhood, living at home with no hope of anything more. Then this gregarious, charming hunk of a man knocks on her door. Not only that, but he sees something in her. He wants her.

It's not the kind of upheaval just anyone can pull off. Even someone as talented as Willa. I try to believe she understands what it might be like. But then we come to the scene where Starbuck kisses Lizzie, and I know she doesn't get it. She moves into the kiss like a seasoned actress, not a timid spinster with low self-esteem. I almost hop up onstage to show her how it's done.

But I don't.

I'm not that good of an actress. It's taken about three rehearsals for my attraction to Andy to turn into a full-blown crush. Adding to my struggle: I still don't know if he's married. No ring and he hasn't said a word about a wife or kids, but I've learned the hard way not to take too much stock in what a guy doesn't say ... or wear. He always hurries out the door as soon as I dismiss them.

We've only really talked a few times, but it was enough to know he is witty and smart and nice. And not "what-a-nice-guy" nice. Good-nice. He encourages everyone, offers advice, and spends much of his limited down-time helping Ron learn his lines.

But the clincher happened right before our third rehearsal started, when Andy asked if we could say a quick prayer. A few cast members politely declined while the rest of us stood in a circle and held hands as Andy thanked God for the fun opportunity and the great cast and wrapped it up by asking Him to bless our endeavors.

That's when I fell. Crashed to the ground like a chopped tree.

In most respects, though, Andy is still a mystery. What he does for a living, how he spends his weekends, who he hangs out with, where he stands on deeper spiritual matters like church and biblical authority—I don't have a clue. And if things don't change soon, the show will be over, he'll go his way and I'll go mine and that will be that.

I so don't want that to be that.

But what can I do? I can't just walk up to him and ask if he's married.

As we finish our second Thursday night rehearsal, I remind everyone I expect them to be off-book by Monday and we all say good night. Then Merle takes off, mumbling something about how he promised his wife he'd be home by nine and it was already five after. Everyone's leaving and the lights are still on. It's the first time I've been alone in the theatre since the light incident almost two weeks before.

What can I say? I panic like a high school girl in a horror movie.

"Andy!"

He turns around, almost to the lobby doors. "Yeah?"

"I, um. Could you ... stay while I turn off the lights and lock up?"

He starts toward me. Moseying, of course. Then he grins. "You're not scared, are you?"

"No." *Yes.* "But what if I am?"

"No one could blame you."

"It's an eerie place."

"With a ghost."

"Yes." I grin at him. "It has a ghost."

We walk backstage and turn off the lights. The darkness settles around us. He feels so close. He smells so good. Not like cologne but a nice, crisp, clean laundry kind of smell. I want to rub my nose in his shirt.

"So," I say, "I feel like I hardly know anything about you."

Andy follows me back onstage and helps me change the set from the act-three arrangement to the act-one set-up we need for Monday. He says,

"What do you want to know?"

"Well, for instance, what do you do for a living?"

"I'm a real estate agent. What about you?"

"Me?" I have a hard time reconciling such an unromantic occupation with the impressive specimen of a man standing in front of me. It's a good career. I was just hoping for something a little more exciting. Like an architect or a U.S. marshal.

Right, Stephie. U.S. marshals always end up performing in community theatre in Bellefontaine, Ohio.

"Yes, you," he says. "You do have a day job, don't you?"

I put my hands on my hips. And wish I was smaller than a size twelve. Wish I was cuter. Wonder if he likes purple-streaked hair. "Of course I have a ... well, sort of. I'm a freelance marketing specialist."

Andy quirks an eyebrow at me. "Did you just make that up?"

He looks so seriously unserious I have to laugh. "It's a real job, I promise." *Just not a very secure one.* "I also substitute teach and take on other short-term jobs as they come along. I mean, I make decent money, most of the time—"

Stop talking.

"But I have to be careful, money-wise, and I'm glad they're paying me for this, though it's not really all that—"

Please stop talking.

And, finally, I do.

Which makes Andy ask, "It's not what?"

"It doesn't pay a whole lot." I sling my purse over my shoulder and pick up my script and notebook. We head toward the exit. I don't have any more excuses to draw the evening out. Besides, he probably wants to get home to his wife.

I sigh, just as a stage light flicks on.

Oh bother. Not again.

We both stop and look at the stage.

Andy says, "Didn't we turn all the lights off?"

"Pretty sure."

"We must have missed one." He heads back to the front. "You wait here. I'll get it."

He's halfway there when the light snaps off again.

Andy glances back at me. "That was weird."

"Uh huh."

He starts toward me, pauses when he sees what I'm sure isn't the most nonchalant expression on my face, and his eyes widen. "Oh, wait. You think it's your ghost, Juniper."

"She's not *my* ghost."

"But that's why you wanted me to stay."

"Well—"

"And here I thought it was because you had a thing for me."

This, of course, immediately causes my heart to stop beating. He stares down at me, grinning like a cat with a mouse.

That's when half of the security lights click off. I can still see him, caught in the dim glow coming from the entrance hall behind me. So close. Close and cute and full-on Starbuck. I almost expect him to tell me to admit I'm pretty, just like in the play.

But he does say, his voice low and a little hoarse, "I think she likes me."

"Who?"

He laughs. "Your ghost."

"She's not my—"

And he kisses me. He grabs me by the shoulders and plants one. Firm but soft and completely awkward.

It's so unexpected and perfect and too soon but too late that I can barely take it in. I don't have a chance to kiss him back before he lifts his head. One second and it's over. I stumble a bit and grasp his arm. All I can think to say is,

"Are you married?" Apparently, I *can* just up and ask him.

He chuckles. Deep and teasing. "No. Are you?"

"Definitely not." Though I try to keep the regret and hurt out of my voice, I suspect he hears both.

For several seconds—a lifetime, if not longer—we stare at each other. As I watch, his expression changes, from open and interested to closed and uncertain. His hands drop from my shoulders, and he takes a step back and says,

"Stephie, I'm ... sorry about that. I'm not really sure why I kissed you."

"That's okay."

"No, it's not. I mean, I don't want you to get the wrong idea."

Well, here we go.

He says, "I'm not—"

"I know."

"I just don't think we should—"

"It's all right, Andy. I ... don't expect anything. Sometimes these things just happen."

Always. Not sometimes. These things just happen to me *always*.

Chapter 4
Juniper

The Wellesleys offered to drive Juniper home so her parents could leave early. Juniper needed to stay and mingle and Mrs. Wellesley needed to wax eloquent over every act of the night and admire every evening gown of every woman she knew. And as the wife of beloved Bellefontaine physician Dr. Horace Wellesley, Anna Wellesley knew every woman in town. This meant they were at the theatre until the manager locked the door behind them.

But Juniper was, at last, seated in the backseat of the Wellesleys' Chevrolet as they motored toward her house. Normally, she'd be sitting and chatting with the Wellesley's daughter—and her dearest friend—Coraletta, but Cora was home with a fever. Tonight, though, Juniper was almost glad she didn't have to say a word.

She clutched a stunning bouquet of red roses to her chest, aware of the thorn on one of the stems that scratched at her skin just above the neckline of her dress, but too weary to do anything about it. As it was, she was trying her best to pay attention to Mrs. Wellesley's effervescent gushing over Juniper's performance. The pricking thorn, in point of fact, helped her stay focused on what the good-hearted, if rather flighty, woman was saying.

"Delightful, my dear," Mrs. Wellesley declared for the hundredth time. "And so heartfelt!" The older woman looked back over her shoulder from where she sat next to her husband in their new Ford. "How do you know so much about lost loves, dear?"

Juniper was grateful for the ride, but she longed for silence. Fortunately, Mrs. Wellesley never expected an answer. She only stopped talking long enough to draw a breath and, every once in a while, to let her husband insert a quip or question of his own. He had a biting sense of humor, and his wife always had a quick response. If her mood had been better, Juniper would have enjoyed the ride and their banter so much more.

As it was, she'd basically forgotten most of what was said five minutes after getting home. Once the Wellesleys dropped her off at her parents' house, all she wanted to do was go to bed. But her mother met her at the door, grabbed her by the hand, and pulled her into the back parlor.

"I've already received almost half a dozen phone calls about your performance, dear, and the Methodist Ladies' Aid Society wants you to sing at their Christmas benefit."

"They do?"

"Now, we'll want to start putting together your repertoire right away."

"Oh, not tonight, Mother. Please. I'm exhausted."

Mrs. Remington clicked her tongue much like she did when feeding the chickens and held up Juniper's arms to her sides like a cross, examining the silky, backless white sheath she wore. "This dress is perfectly lovely, but we should do something different with your hair."

Juniper held back a groan. "But that's months away. Can't we talk about it in the morning so I can go to bed now? Please?" She tried to give her mother an "aren't-I-cute?" look but suspected she just looked pinched and pained.

Her mother stepped back and studied her face. She didn't smile. "Junie, you need to stop acting like bad things happen *to* you."

"But ... they do."

Martha Remington smoothed a hand over Juniper's softly waving brown hair. "No, dear. Bad things just happen. To everyone. You're only a victim if you make yourself one."

"William's gone, Mother, and I'll never see him again. That happened *to* me. And because of me."

"Don't be ridiculous. It's not your fault."

Juniper turned away. "Yes, it is," she whispered. She'd never been able to tell her mother the whole story of why William left. Martha thought he simply wasn't in love with her. And he wasn't. Not enough anyway. But there was more to it: William believed her family was beneath him. If only Juniper had been clever enough or alluring enough to convince him she was worth it.

So here she was. An old maid at twenty-two. Living with her parents. Singing at ladies' society meetings. Could it be enough? Could she be happy?

She should pray and seek God's guidance. It would help.

Maybe. Or maybe not.

Instead she went to bed and cried herself to sleep.

Chapter 5
Stephie

Because we're both so used to acting, Andy and I are able to pretend nothing has happened to change our director-actor relationship. I try not to think about how strong his lips felt against mine or wonder why he tasted like Pepsi when I've never seen him drink anything at rehearsals other than Tim Horton's coffee or bottled water.

But I put all that behind me and concentrate on getting *The Rainmaker* ready for opening night.

Then, the Monday after Halloween, less than three weeks before the show is to start, I get a call from Geoffrey Barnes, Willa's husband. Geoffrey, not Geoff. Willa insists everyone call him Geoffrey. Maybe he prefers it too. Who knows? I doubt Willa ever asked him.

Anyway, he calls me at nine that morning while I'm looking for costume pieces at Goodwill and, with barely a "hello," blurts out the news that Willa was in an accident the day before. Which immediately causes me to have a minor breakdown next to piles of belts and shelves of shoes.

"What happened? Is she okay?"

"We were hiking the caves at Hocking Hills and, well, she tripped on a tree root and broke her foot."

"Oh, ouch. How is she?"

A breath that sounds rather frustrated vibrates the airwaves. "The doctor says she'll be fine eventually but … I'm sorry, Stephie. She can't walk. She's supposed to stay off her foot as much as possible."

I sure wish men would stop apologizing to me for stuff they can't—or won't—change.

"If she needs to miss a few rehearsals or wear a cast, I understand."

"Actually, she asked me to let you know she's going to have to drop out of the play."

"Wait. What? She can't do it at all?"

"I'm afraid not. She might need surgery."

I take a deep breath and try to calm myself down. "Lizzie could have a cast. We could just make it part of the show."

He laughs. "Willa actually suggested that but the doctor said he didn't even want her standing up long enough to do the dishes. Lucky me."

"But … what am I supposed to do? Where am I going to find someone who can pick up the part in three weeks?"

Even as I speak, though, I know exactly who can and will play Lizzie. But Geoffrey and Willa—especially Willa—don't need to know that.

"Sorry, Stephie," he says again, only this time I don't mind. "I hope everything works out."

And the line drops dead.

So. I'll have to do it, of course. Who else could jump in at such a late date? I would be

Lizzie. I swallow down a giggle. No one should rejoice in another person's pain.

But I do let myself smile a little. Then I turn toward Goodwill's hat section to see if they have a 1930s-era straw bonnet that happens to fit me.

❊ ❊ ❊

That night, I bring a card for everyone to sign to include with the flowers I plan to send Willa. But I'm in a room full of men, and they don't seem all that concerned about needing a new actress. Still, someone does ask who I plan to replace Willa with.

I say, "I thought that, maybe—since we don't have many options at such a late date—I could play Lizzie. Would you all be okay with that?"

They shrug and nod and Andy says, "Sure, why not?"

They don't exactly lift me up on their shoulders and carry me triumphantly onto the stage, but they don't dump all over the idea either. One of the benefits of a mostly male cast. I put Merle in charge as we jump right into act one, scene one, and run through the whole thing, beginning to end. It flows much more smoothly than I expected. And I only need Merle to throw me a handful of lines.

But when the time comes for Starbuck to kiss Lizzie, Andy brushes the corner of my mouth with his lips in what I would label "brotherly" at best. It will never do, and we don't have time for him to be shy. He hadn't had that problem with Willa. Besides, the man can kiss.

Can he ever. And I still have the goose bumps to prove it.

I don't know how to bring it up, though, so I let it go, figuring it can wait. If things don't improve, I'll have to say something. Which causes me to spend the twenty-four hours before the next rehearsal hashing it out and hoping and praying he'll man up and get it done.

Because all I can come up with is, "Remember how you kissed me the other night? Yeah, do that again." Which wouldn't be awkward at all.

Turns out, I fretted for nothing. Our second rehearsal as Lizzie and Starbuck is pure magic. He falls into his part so completely, in that moment I'm not Stephie and he's not Andy and the kiss is perfect and passionate. I ask Merle later how it looked to him and he says,

"Well, the two of you have chemistry all right."

"So, it works?"

"Like Bogie and Bacall."

If that had come from someone else, I would have worried he was just being nice or I'd have pushed for more feedback. But coming from

Merle, that's high praise and I know we're on the right track.

At Thursday's rehearsal, I bring homemade chocolate chip cookies and creamy vanilla ice cream. It's supposed to be our last run-through before we start full-blown dress and set and lighting and sound rehearsals on Monday. I'm ready to celebrate.

Then, of course, everything falls apart. People miss entrances, forget lines, and phone in their performances. Even the characterizations we've been working on for seven weeks are off. Not just off. The whole show is a dozen shades of blah. Everyone just seems bored. So before Merle even gets to the rehearsal notes, I announce my intention to have an extra rehearsal on Saturday or Sunday.

"I don't care what time or which day," I say. "We need it."

After some discussion, we settle on Saturday morning at ten. The men file out but, to my surprise, Andy lags behind. Since the night I'd asked him to stay and we had our little moment, he hasn't raced out the door as quickly but seems to wait to see if Merle is staying to help me lock up. Most of the time, Merle does and Andy leaves. But this night, Andy strolls to the back to take care of the lights while I set the stage for Saturday.

Once we're done, without any interference from lights or troublesome spirits, he starts toward the exit while I gather all my stuff together. Then he stops, turns, and comes back.

"Are you hungry?"

"Hungry?"

"Yeah, I was thinking I might go get something to eat. And some company would be nice."

I smile. "Don't you have to work tomorrow?"

He grins back, hooking his thumbs in his belt buckles, reminding me of John Wayne and the first time he swaggered into my life almost two months ago. "Fridays are a bit more flexible at my office and I don't have any appointments until ten."

"What did you have in mind?"

"Pizza at Six Hundred? We could just walk over."

"Sounds good."

We step outside, and the November chill slices through me in an icy blast. I run across the street to put everything but my purse in my ancient red Subaru. Andy meets me on the sidewalk and I pull my scarf tighter around my ears as we take the short stroll to the downtown restaurant. Stars and a half-moon light the night sky. It's only eight-thirty, yet the streets are practically deserted. After years of living in Chicago, I'm still not used to the slower pace of small-town Ohio life.

I like it, but I'm not used to it.

We don't say much as we walk; it's possible Andy is as cold as I am. He hunches over in his leather jacket, his hands stuffed in his pockets. Our breaths come out in wisps of frosty air. I would have been more excited about finally arriving at the restaurant if not for the fact we'll have to walk back to our cars later. When it will be that much colder. Good thing we chose a place barely a block from the theatre.

Andy opens the door, and we hurry inside the renowned pizzeria, called Six Hundred because that's the temperature at which they bake pizzas in their old-fashioned brick oven. The appealing scent of sauce and cheese and baked dough surrounds me, igniting my taste buds, and my stomach responds. I guess I am hungry. Though I can always eat pizza. So I gratefully let Andy hang up my coat and lead me to a booth in the corner. He settles in across from me.

Though it's not quite Thanksgiving yet, the restaurant is draped in Christmas colors and soft twinkle lights. I clear my throat to stop myself from saying something silly about how incredibly romantic it is.

A petite waitress with thick, curly, dark hair and Chinese letters tattooed on her wrist bounces over.

"Welcome to Six Hundred," she says with enough enthusiasm for all of us. "I'm Emily. Can I get you something to drink?"

She hands us menus as we both ask for water, sans ice. I would have preferred hot chocolate to warm me from the inside, but it's not on the menu. They don't have cream soda either. So water it is. Emily returns with our drinks, and we order a large chicken barbecue pizza.

Then we sit there in silence, sipping water and staring at the pictures on the walls. I run through my lines from the play in my head and wish someone would write a script for my life. For this moment anyway. That way I'd have something brilliant and delightful to say, and he would laugh and fall heels over head for me. You can write any two people in love in a story. It's not so easy in real life. Even when that real life includes a tall, sweet man who can make you forget your own name with one kiss.

If only that moment made things easier now. But here we sit, pretending it never happened and that we actually want to be lounging in a restaurant sharing a friendly silence because we don't need words.

Yeah, right.

Finally, he breaks the quiet with some questions about the show. It's all pretty theatre-related until he asks, "Do you live here in Bellefontaine?"

"Yes, I have a little apartment a few blocks down the street from the hospital. You?"

"My family has a farm near Indian Lake."

I take a sip of water. "You live with your family?"

"Near them. My parents are in the main house, but I have my own place on the other side of the hill. And my sister and her family live just down the road."

"Sounds nice."

"It is. We're pretty close." He tugs on his earlobe, then, "What about your family? Are they around here?"

"My family?" Shoot. I'm about to out-and-out lie when Emily saves the day by showing up with our pizza, setting the pie on an empty restaurant-sized tomato sauce can in the middle of the table.

I gnaw down a few bites, swallow politely, and, just in case he wants to return to the subject, throw in, "I have a cat."

"Oh yeah?"

"Yeah." I scoop a piece of cheese from my plate and lick it off my finger. "Wait, don't tell me—you're allergic. Seems like everyone is nowadays."

"No. We have four or five at the farm."

"You're not sure?"

"Well, they come and go." He laughs. "It's more like we belong to them than the other way around."

"I know what you mean. Cozy likes to let me know who's in charge."

"Cozy?"

"Short for Cosette, from Les Mis."

"Cute."

I snag a second slice, relieved. I have successfully changed the subject. I can eat in peace. Which of course is when he says, "So, you were going to tell me about your family."

Gulp. "I was?"

"You weren't?"

"Well … there's not much to tell."

He waits. Chews. Smiles.

"I … um … don't technically have one."

He leans back. "You don't have one? How do you not have a family?"

"A woman found me when I was a newborn, screaming in an alley behind a high school in Chicago. I grew up in the foster system." I shrug, like that's a life history people tell all the time. I don't mention the years of wondering why no one wanted me. "So, no parents, no siblings, no aunts or uncles."

For what seems like hours, he sits there like a statue, staring at me. Okay, I don't look like an orphan. Then again, what does an orphan look like? Annie? Pollyanna? Even Pollyanna eventually grew up. It's obvious Andy doesn't have a clue how to respond to this revelation. Poor fellow. I should at least try to make it easy on him.

"It's not as traumatic as it sounds. I had several decent foster parents and one really good one and, well, God has taken care of me. Besides, don't they say what doesn't kill you makes you stronger?"

"You seem strong."

"You bet I am. Most of the time." At his look I continue, "Holidays can be rough, but I've had thirty-seven years to figure out how to make it work."

"Did you grow up in Chicago?"

Since I now have a mouth full of pizza, I hold up a pause finger and he nods, taking a bite himself while he waits. It's so tasty, I savor it a bit before saying, "I did. Lived there until I moved here three years ago."

"Really." He seems genuinely intrigued. What an unusual man. "How on earth did you end up in Bellefontaine?"

"Hmm, well, that's a long story and it's getting late." I take out my wallet and set a twenty percent tip on the table. Deciding it's worth a shot, I grin as casually as possible and ask, "Rain check?"

He scowls at me. Tilts his head. "I hate rain checks. Don't have the patience for them."

Ha. "I know what you mean. But seriously, I'd kind of like you to get used to the whole idea of me being an orphan before getting into the rest of my story. Besides, my journey to Bellefontaine isn't nearly so interesting. Trust me. One why-I'm-so-messed-up revelation at a time is enough."

More than enough.

Then Andy says, "Would you want to get together for lunch after rehearsal Saturday? You could tell me then."

I don't even pause for a micro-second. "Yeah, that would be great. But you have to tell me one of your issues too. If we're going to be friends, you have to be at least a little messed up."

He seems surprised and amused. "Okay. I think I can meet that criteria. So … Saturday?"

"Sounds good."

Saturday. Just two nights without sleep.

I can manage.

Chapter 6
Juniper

Later the next day, Peter Billings came to call. Juniper couldn't remember a time when they weren't friends. She couldn't possibly take him seriously, though; he lived for baseball and goofing around with his friends at the jelly joint, drinking root beer and throwing peanut shells on the floor. Still, he had a knack for lightening the day, and her mood.

"Hiya, sweetheart," he said, chucking her under the chin. "I heard you were aces at the show last night."

All she could do was smile and invite him in. "I did all right."

"Ah, don't kid a kidder." Then he grinned. "After all, I was there."

"What? Now who's kidding?" She led him into the parlor. "I didn't see you."

Peter almost fell onto the sofa, crossed his legs at the ankles and leaned back like he owned the place. "I didn't want you to see me."

"Congratulations. I didn't." Juniper settled into a wingback chair near the fireplace and crossed her own ankles in a more acceptable and genteel fashion. She didn't look at him. Sometimes Peter's silly games seemed nothing more than tiresome and childish. Why couldn't he just grow up?

"Well?" he said. "Aren't you going to ask me?"

Juniper sighed. "Ask you what, Peter?"

"Why I didn't want you to see me."

"What difference does it make?"

"Oh, uh …" He suddenly seemed uncertain, like he hadn't expected such a reaction. But he said, "I thought it would make things easier for you."

"Really?" Juniper smoothed her hands down her navy-blue pencil skirt. He was like a boy offering her a lollipop. How could he possibly know what would make things easier for her? Could he go to New York and bring William back?

"Sure. I didn't want to make you nervous when you saw me out there."

Which only made her laugh. "Oh, Peter, when have you ever made me nervous?"

He lowered his voice to almost a whisper. "I could make you nervous."

She took a breath that probably sounded as frustrated as she felt. "Why did you come over?"

"To see you."

"Peter."

"What? You know how I feel."

As if on cue, her mother chose that moment to flounce into the room. Few people could flounce like Martha Remington. "Ah, there you are, dear." She turned to their guest. "Peter. Lovely to see you. How is your father?"

"He's getting along. The doctor told him to take it easy for a few weeks."

"I'd say, at the very least." Mother shook her head, her eyes sad. "A heart attack is nothing to take lightly."

Peter smiled. "No, ma'am."

"Tell your mother I'll come by tomorrow with fresh bread and some of last year's tomato jam. It's my best to date." At Peter's nod, Martha turned to Juniper. "Your father and I are supping with the Wellesleys tonight. You can heat up the rest of the macaroni casserole for dinner. And there's plenty for Peter, if he wants to join you. I'm sure he's hungry after a hard day's labor."

"I sure am, Mrs. Remington. Though it wasn't that hard of a day." With a grin, Peter looked at Juniper, his sky-blue eyes lit with hope. "If it's okay with Junie, I'd be keen to stay."

"Of course," Juniper said. "Don't be dingy."

Martha shook her head. "Well, I take it that means 'yes.' I don't know why you kids have to be constantly making up new words when we already have more than we need, but I'll leave you to it."

After she had gone, Peter followed Juniper into the kitchen, where she put the casserole in the oven. She leaned against the counter and watched him for a moment. He really was ridiculously cute, with his shaggy hair and ready smile. When he wasn't being so off the cob, anyway.

So she said, "I just can't take you seriously, Peter."

"Why not?"

"Because you don't take anything seriously. You have no ambition."

He crossed his arms on his chest and tried to harrumph, though it wasn't as effective as one of her father's growls. "For your information, I have a great job with plenty of potential."

"You're a shoe salesman."

"I'm in retail with an eye on a management position."

Juniper tilted her head and pursed her lips. She didn't like word games. "Don't give yourself airs. You're still just a shoe salesman."

"And a snazzy one at that."

He grinned and Juniper groaned inwardly. This wasn't getting them anywhere. Maybe she just needed to be blunt.

After about an hour of honesty and arguing, Peter finally stomped away, taking his broken heart with him. He slammed the door on his way out, making Juniper jump half out of her skin. She hadn't handled that well at all but knew he'd get over it eventually.

"I guess everyone's disappointed in love," she whispered. Maybe that's just the way things were.

With her stomach still growling, Juniper turned toward the casserole she'd pulled out of the oven half an hour before. The once-bubbly cheese sauce was now lukewarm and had congealed on the top.

But she ate some anyway. After a few bites on a suddenly sour stomach, though, she discovered her appetite was sorely wanting. With nothing else to distract her, she cleaned up the kitchen and went to bed.

Chapter 7
Stephie

Everyone shows up for Saturday's rehearsal in costume, as I had requested, and we fly through it. The improvement over Thursday night is so phenomenal, I can't stop smiling. Until Andy comes up to me afterward and tells me he forgot his fourteen-year-old nephew has a basketball tournament at one this afternoon and he promised to be there. I barely have time to be disappointed when he adds,

"So, do you want to come? It's in Marysville. We could grab subs on the way."

"Um, yeah. Sure."

"We probably won't get back until, like, eight or so. Is that okay?"

It briefly occurs to me to hesitate. To say I have plans tonight. To not be that girl without a social life. But what's the chance he'd believe that?

So I say, "That's not a problem."

I follow Andy out to his mud-encrusted, black Jeep and hop in. We stop for subs—chipotle steak for Andy, turkey and provolone for me—then head east on 33. I almost ordered tuna but decided it wasn't a good idea when eating in a confined space. I sometimes wish I'd stop worrying about making a good impression and just relax and enjoy myself. A psychiatrist, I'm sure, would have something to say about that.

But, really, I'm with a man I'm attracted to, and I don't want to turn him off with strong odors. Is that so wrong?

We eat in relative silence as Andy steers the Jeep toward Marysville. I consider a dozen things to ask him on the way but swallow each question down for one reason or another. Worst of all, I feel a gnawing desperation for him to like me. This happens a lot when I'm interested in someone and usually means I will, in the end, push him away. So I dig down deep for some measure of normality, say a quick prayer, and remind myself that even if things don't work out with Andy, I'll still be fine.

Alone, but fine. Like always.

When we arrive at the high school where the tournament is being held, I realize it's quite the event. The place swarms with kids and adults, yet Andy makes a beeline for a far corner of the gym, where about twenty people immediately surround him.

A woman, not much older than me, grabs his arm. "It's about time! Jordan's second game is about to start."

Andy glances around the gym, then waves at a gangly, red-haired kid who grins and waves back. Andy asks the woman, "How did the first game go?"

"It was close but they eked out a win." She smiles at me, looks at Andy, and tilts her head. In that moment, I definitely see the resemblance. She asks how our rehearsal went.

"Fine," he says, his eyes on the basketball court.

With a grunt, the woman sticks out her hand toward me. "Well, if my brother can't take care of introductions, I'll do it. I'm Brenda."

"Oh, sorry." His tone tells me he really isn't. "Brenda, this is Stephie, our director. Stephie, meet my pushy, older sister."

"Pushy!" Brenda laughs. "The correct word is 'assertive.' And somebody has to be around here." We shake hands and she says, "Brothers. Do you have any, Stephie?"

Andy clears his throat, and a line of red splotches up the side of his neck.

"No," I say. "No brothers."

Brenda chuckles again. "Lucky. You want mine?"

I'm not sure how she misses it but, somehow, Brenda doesn't catch the tension radiating off of said brother. Poor guy. He hasn't a clue how to handle this. So I say,

"Oh, I couldn't do that to you. We all have to accept our lot in life."

Laughing, Brenda introduces me to more of Andy's family: his parents, of course, and Brenda's husband, Tom, along with the rest of their children. I count at least half a dozen. I might have missed a few. Then we take our seats on the bleachers, eat popcorn, drink ice cold cans of cola, and watch Jordan's team win three more games, making it to the final four before being taken out by a team that, to me, looked decidedly older. Definitely taller. Still, the grins sported by Jordan and his friends tell me they consider it a successful day.

Throughout the series of games, I spend more time chatting with Brenda than Andy, in between cheers. Someone that easy to talk to doesn't come along every day. She has a great sense of humor and we talk so much I barely have a chance to catch my breath. By the time Jordan's last game ends, I know most of her life story and she even knows quite a bit about me. Which is why, with very little prying, I relent and tell her my family history. Or lack of one.

She leans her chin on her hand and stares at me with the same intense expression Andy had when he heard the story. Again, I notice the family resemblance. Especially in the deep green of their eyes.

Finally, she says, "Oh, so that's why Andy was all sweaty when I asked if you had brothers."

"That's why."

A smile lifts the corner of her mouth. "Are you sure you don't want him?"

I chew on a fingernail and glance over at where Andy stands on the sidelines, talking with his dad and ruffling Jordan's spiky hair. "I might."

"Yeah, I thought so."

When I look at her grinning face, she shrugs. "It had to happen eventually. Even for a giant schlub like my brother."

"Schlub?"

"Oh, he's a schlub. Trust me."

"Okay." Now it's my turn to laugh. "I don't know what that is."

Her dad—I already forgot his name—calls up to us from the front of the bleachers, "Brenda! Steph! Come on. We're taking the kids to Benny's for pizza."

Pizza? Twice in three days? Well ... why not?

I turn to join them and Brenda puts a hand on my arm. "He likes you too, Stephie."

"Hmm." I look at her. I glance around the gym. I do not look at him. "I'm not so sure about that." My voice cracks, despite every effort to sound easy-going. *Not even close to breezy, Stephie.*

"Well, I could be wrong." She wiggles her eyebrows like we're co-conspirators. "But I'm not."

Can I believe her? I want to. But I have a history and great guys like Andy wanting to share my life never seem to become a part of it.

This, however, doesn't stop me from letting hope bubble and spread its heat through the center of my chest. If Starbuck can fall for Lizzie, why can't Andy fall for me? So I push aside the reminder that *The Rainmaker* is a work of fiction. All fiction has some basis in fact, right?

Eventually, I believe, things can change. So I ride with Andy to Benny's, cozy up to him as much as possible at the crowded table, laugh at his liberal use of red pepper flakes, and let myself imagine what it might be like to be a part of the Tremont family.

All the way home, we talk and laugh and I know, if nothing else, we're friends. I say, "So, do you think you'll participate in future Holland Theatre productions?"

"You bet."

"But if you've lived here all your life, why is this your first show?"

"Well, I grew up here, but I moved to Columbus for college. It's when I was at Ohio State that I really caught the acting bug."

"Oh, right. You told us about your performances there at auditions."

"Yep. I've only been back here for a few years and this is the first time I've been able to audition." He glances at me with an easy smile. "And I really wanted to play Starbuck."

"I'm glad you did."

"By the way ..." He pauses so long I wonder if he forgot what he wanted to say. Then, "You wanted to know my ... issue."

"No. That's okay. I was just kidding around."

"Yeah? Well, I'm gonna tell you anyway."

I brace myself. Reach up and grab the handle over the door. Then I realize how awkward that looks and rub my hand on my jeans. "If you want."

"All right." He takes a deep breath. "I haven't been in a serious relationship since college."

I find that hard to believe.

He continues, "That's surprising, I guess—"

Mind reader.

"—but I had a bad relationship and I've been pretty jumpy about the whole thing ever since."

"What happ—" Then I hold up my hand. "No. You don't have to tell me." We're back in Bellefontaine and he pulls up next to where I left my car at the theatre.

Andy puts the Jeep in park and turns to me. "She broke my heart. In a nutshell."

"I'm sorry."

"I suppose it's not that unusual."

"No, it's not." I shift sideways and lean my head against the seat as I study him. It's so quiet; I don't even hear cars on Main Street. Of course, it's after ten. But it's also a Saturday night. A nearby streetlight flickers off and I wonder, for a moment, if Juniper has access to that switch too.

Who cares? I want to feel closer to him. Emotionally and spiritually, if not physically. Again, I catch his clean, masculine scent.

"I like your hair that way." He whispers it, as if he, too, likes the intimacy of the moment.

"You do?" I smooth my bangs from my forehead. I dyed it back to my natural, dirty blonde color. Lizzie couldn't very well have lavender-streaked hair back in the 1930s. "I thought it looked kind of bland."

"Stephie, the last thing you will ever be is bland."

We sit there for a few moments longer. I'm aware of his breathing and how the sound competes with the strong winter winds whipping around us outside. I'm not looking forward to having to leave the warmth of his truck for my cold car. Finally, I say,

"Well, I guess I should go."

"All right. Good night."

I sigh but don't move. "Good night."

Then he chuckles. "Do you want to stay?"

"No." But I nod.

"So stay."

So I do. We talk for another hour about life and movies and dreams and theatre. I honestly don't remember anything specific. But when I finally scurry to my car, I'm happy.

Chapter 8
Juniper

Three months after Peter stormed out of her house, Juniper stood in the Holland Theatre's dressing room, preparing for her latest performance, a holiday benefit arranged by the Ladies' Aid Society. She hadn't talked with him since that night and, even more remarkable, had actually convinced herself that was a good thing. Now, as she painted her lips cherry red and scrolled through her song repertoire in her head, she mentally stopped herself at least half a dozen times from slipping upstairs and searching the audience.

For Peter.

Mercy. Why was she still thinking about him? He was just a boy. A cute and funny and ambitionless boy. He couldn't fulfill her dreams. Nothing about Bellefontaine, Ohio, could make her dreams come true.

She needed to leave this town. That had become crystal clear over the last few months. If she could just get to New York. To Broadway.

To William. Surely he would take her back. He would see her and recognize her unstoppable ambition and want her again. She could picture them together in New York, taking over the big city with charm and finesse. William had the skill to revive Wall Street; Juniper would shine on the stage. Tucking a curl into place on her forehead, she sighed.

You can't build a life on a dream, Junie.

Still, as she primped it occurred to her that the dream had lost some of its charm. Did she really want to chase after a man who had rejected her so coldly? Did she want to chase after a man at all? What if she showed up on his doorstep, only to have him turn her away? The thought sent a chill through her.

Footsteps on the stairs broke Juniper's reverie. Martha Remington came through the door, grinning and carrying a corsage box.

"Dear, you look stunning," she said. "Are you about ready?"

"Yes, Mother, I think so."

"Wonderful!" Her mother pulled a white gardenia corsage out of the box. It was lovely. She carefully pinned it to Juniper's sleek, red gown. "Your father and I decided you needed something special and so I ordered this. Isn't it perfectly beautiful?"

Catching a whiff of the flower's delicate scent, Juniper breathed it in. It soothed her spirit. "Yes," she whispered. "It's perfect."

Mother fussed over Juniper's dress and hair, smoothing and curling and patting things into place. Then she said, "I saw Peter in the lobby," and Juniper's heart momentarily stilled.

Gathering her thoughts from where they had suddenly scattered throughout the room, she said, "Peter's here? He came to the show?"

"Of course, dear. Why wouldn't he? I've never seen a boy so smitten."

"Oh, Mother." She took another deep breath. What difference did it make? It was too late for anything now.

But when she stepped on to the stage, she chose not to think about—or sing for—William.

Chapter 9
Stephie

I love Tech Week. It's always been my favorite part of a production. Seeing all of our hard work finally come together with costumes and lights and sound never fails to thrill me. And this show couldn't be more exciting. When Andy first walks into his scene in his suspenders and rakishly tilted straw hat, the swig of cream soda I've just taken attacks my throat and I cough and sputter for a good five minutes. Merle, always on-hand to help out, slaps me on the back, which shakes me up and hurts a little but doesn't make things better. So I suffer 'til my eyes water.

Once I can talk again, I ask the actors to take their places. After going over announcements and notes and whatever else is on my mind, I join them onstage.

The hardest part is being under the lights instead of enjoying the magic from the audience. Something I didn't take into consideration when I leaped like a trout into the role. Oh well. It just means I can never stop moving. Every time I'm offstage, I run to the back of the auditorium to check with Kelvin, our sound guy, and Janeane, who does lights, or slip into the wings backstage to chat with our stage manager, Trish, about props and curtains and any tiny costume pieces we might still need. Merle, meanwhile, keeps his eyes on everything taking place in the scene.

We wrap up late Monday night. With only three more rehearsals until we open, I can feel the pressure, like hands on my shoulders, pushing me down. I am reassuring myself with deep breaths after almost everyone has left, when Merle turns to me and says,

"I'm just not sure it's enough."

"Enough what?" I clear my throat, hoping and praying that scratchy taste is damage from the cream soda incident, not an indication I have a virus that will rise up on angry hind legs and mutilate my dream of a smooth performance.

"Enough income to keep things going."

I turn to him. "What are you talking about?"

Once again Merle looks at me as if he has serious doubts as to my intelligence level. Then he sighs. "I'm talking about the buy-out. Come on, Stephanie."

Now it's my turn to give the look. "Merle, I haven't heard about any buy-out. Could you just tell me what's going on?"

"All right." He adjusts in his chair so he can face me directly. Merle doesn't like to turn his head. "If we don't make enough with this show, the board is considering selling the theatre to a developer."

I lean back, so thrown off I'm glad I'm sitting. A developer means one thing: no more theatre.

They'll tear it down and put in a parking lot or another Speedway or a cheap apartment complex. I swallow my frustration with Merle and realize the feeling in my throat is worse. If I don't get some immune support drugs in me soon, I won't have a voice by opening night. I say,

"Why didn't you tell me? I would have done something else, like *My Fair Lady* or *Scrooge*. Musicals are always better money-makers than straight plays."

Merle shrugs. "To be honest, I don't think it would have mattered. A few of the board members think upkeeping the place costs more money than it's worth."

"How could anyone think that?" I stand and stride up onto the stage. Raising my arms, I turn in a slow circle, studying my home away from home. "This can't possibly be anything but a theatre. And it should be treated as a vital part of the community."

With a sigh, I glance around, trying to imagine it gone. The Holland truly is an amazing, historic structure. To add to its charm, the theatre's massive, two-story walls are painted to look like a 17th-century Dutch cityscape. The buildings are mostly two-dimensional but dimly lit from within. Two large, moving windmills add just the right touch. When I glance up, a twinkling of stars wink back from the ceiling. The Holland Theatre is a one-of-a-kind piece of history that should not be torn down. Which is exactly what I tell Merle.

"I know," he says. "I have many fond memories of hanging out here with friends back in the 50s, watching William Holden and John Wayne fight the Nazis." He rubs the back of his neck and looks around the building, much like I had just done. "There's a lot of history here. Would be a shame to see it torn down."

"So? Can we do anything about it?"

"Like what?"

"I don't know, but we have to try." I pace in front of the stage. The lights in one of the fake Dutch buildings flicker and I wonder if Juniper agrees with me. "What about a fundraiser?"

"It's a great idea, Stephanie. But, to be honest, I think it's too late."

The whole thing is starting to chafe my hide a bit. "That's the plan, isn't it? Keep it on the down-low until it's too late for the community to do anything about it." I stop pacing, trying to ignore my now-sandpaper throat and the pure dread icing through my veins. I need to go home. I need a good night's sleep. I need the show to be so phenomenal this weekend that there will be a town-wide uprising at the thought of shutting the place down.

I need a miracle. But I don't believe in miracles.

Finally, I sit down and sigh. "This stinks."

Merle nods, his thick, white hair moving with the kind of sheen a runway model would envy. "There's a lot of history in this old girl. Juniper would be heartbroken at the thought. She used to sing here, you know."

No, I didn't know. "Really? You mean there actually was a Juniper connected to the Holland?"

"Oh, sure. Juniper Remington. I even heard her sing once. I was five and they had a talent show." He takes a deep breath. "She had the voice of an angel. Looked like one too."

"Wow. So … what happened to her?"

"Hmm." He closes his eyes, as if looking through a photo album of memories. "I don't rightly remember. I think she died young in some kind of accident. Although—"

Merle pauses and I lean toward him. "Although —?"

"Well, there were some who insisted she died of a broken heart. Others said she took her own life. But, as far as I could tell, it was never anything more than gossip. Everyone likes a tragedy."

"True, but it's still sad. I wonder what really happened to her."

"Disappointed in love, I imagine. That's usually the story."

"I suppose." Doesn't make it any less heartbreaking. "Poor Juniper. No wonder she can't let go."

Merle glances at me, concern etching his face, so I add, "No, I don't believe in ghosts. But sometimes you hear a story and you can—almost—understand why a soul would have trouble leaving such great sorrow behind."

"I suppose. Well, if you're really curious, you should ask Cora Wellesley-Jones. Her family and the Remingtons go way back. I imagine she knew Juniper's beau as well."

"The one who broke her heart?"

"Now, that I can't rightly tell you. But Cora could."

❄ ❄ ❄

Of course, I don't have time to talk to Cora this week. Because not only do I get a nasty cold, I have to throw all my energy into the play and several projects clients keep pestering me to complete. In the rush of things, I forget all about Juniper and her sorrows.

I chew on vitamin supplements like they're M&Ms and run warm saline water through my sinuses several times a day. I drink warm lemon and honey tea and pray God will heal me before opening night. But even as I say the words, I doubt the probability. Colds typically hang onto me for weeks at a time, kind of like a hurtful comment.

The night before the show is to open I can't sleep or breathe, so I swallow cold pills and sleep aids and gulp down almost half a bottle of Nyquil. I know it's foolish but all I want is a good night's rest.

When a chilly November sun finally peers through the curtains and nudges me awake, I feel drained. With effort, I crawl out of bed and stumble into the shower, hoping some cool water will wake me up. Halfway through it, a wave of heat and exhaustion washes over me and I have to sit down or pass out. I huddle there, water raining over me until, slowly, a bit of strength returns. Finally, I'm able to step out of the shower and look in the mirror. My face is as white as the snow drifting past my bedroom window.

Apparently, the Holland won't need a ghost over the weekend. It will have me.

Not being the kind of person to ignore illness and hope it will go away, I get dressed, then hurry to my doctor's office for an antibiotic. Yes, it's unlikely they will take effect before the performance tonight but it's a step in the direction of better health. And surely I can fake it for four performances.

I have to. They're counting on me. I don't have a choice.

When I walk into the theatre just before our six o'clock call time that night, every pair of eyes takes on an expression of horror. Andy's the first to speak.

"What happened to you?"

I clear my throat, attempting to lessen the raspy quality of it. "I have a bit of a cold."

"A bit? You look like Typhoid Mary!"

"For your information, Typhoid Mary didn't have typhoid. She just carried the virus."

Andy grunts. He couldn't look more annoyed.

I continue, "So she was never actually sick."

He raises an eyebrow. I've never seen a condescending eyebrow before. Kids these days. Nobody cares about history anymore.

"Besides," I say, "it's not that bad." At least, that's what I try to say. The effort to speak causes me to collapse into a coughing fit that lasts a good minute. I pop in a heavy-duty zinc cough drop, then smile at my cast through watery eyes. "I'll be fine."

Andy moves a step closer, then rethinks it and backs up again. "Um, no. I don't think you will. You shouldn't do this."

I lift my hands. "I have to. It's opening night. We can't cancel the show because of a little cold." Attempting to throw a bit of lightheartedness on the situation, I add, "You know what they say: The show must go on. And it will."

After I take a few steps toward the stage, I turn back to my cast. "But if you're praying people, a few words on my behalf would be appreciated. And please take care of yourselves. One phlegm monster per show is plenty."

They laugh, and I get to work. So much to do to get everything ready and that doesn't include turning me into spinster Lizzie Curry. Fortunately, my friend Ginger is coming by to do my hair so I can save time by applying my makeup then.

But first, I need to find Trish and go over —

Andy taps me on the shoulder, then his hand slides down my arm. That gets my attention.

"Steph, I'm worried about you."

"I appreciate that, Andy, really I do." I put my hand on his arm. Wow. This real estate agent works out. Nice. I hide a sigh behind a breath. "I'll be fine."

"You say that, but I still want to help. So …" He bends his head to gaze right into my eyes. His sparkle like frosty green Christmas lights. Mine probably look more like gray, drippy rain clouds.

But he smiles anyway and asks, "Do you trust me?"

"Trust you? Andy, I don't have time—"

"Just answer the question, Stephie. Do you trust me?"

"Well, yes." I look closer and see my answer reflected in his eyes. "Yes, I trust you."

"Then let me be your director tonight."

Wow. I wish he'd stop being so sweet. "Andy, I can't ask you to do that, you have enough to focus on. You know, playing the lead and all?"

"You're right. I'm onstage a lot." He shrugs. "But I'm a great delegator. I've been watching you keep this show running for eight weeks and I know what needs to be done. So does the rest of the crew, for that matter."

Yes, they could do it. But do I want them to?

"The only real question," Andy says, reading my mind again, "is can you relinquish control of your show?"

No, of course not. It's mine. My work and sweat and ideas. I sneeze and sway a bit, almost knocked over by a wave of dizziness.

He grips my arm to steady me. "Just let it go, Steph. It's all going to be just fine."

And a great sandbag of stress falls from my shoulders and lands with a thud behind me. Then I turn to see Ginger strolling down the right-side aisle toward us. "All right," I tell Andy. "I officially hand the reins to you."

He grins and moseys off. "You won't regret it," he calls over his shoulder.

I turn to Ginger. "I'm all yours, honey."

She shifts her equipment bag from one shoulder to the other and follows me down to "the green room." In reality, it's a damp, cold, creepy, cement-walled room at the bottom of a steep flight of stairs. I refuse to go down there alone but, at the moment, it contains the rest of the cast members, sans Andy. My fellow thespians joke around as they slap on suspenders and apply makeup.

I snatch up my personal makeup bag from the table where I left it earlier and take a seat in an old metal chair in front of a cheap, full-length mirror leaning against the wall. Ginger gets right to work, pulling and tugging and twisting my hair. Since it's barely chin-length, she'll have to add a fake hair piece. I've just started on my foundation when my friend says,

"So, who was that tall drink of water you were talking with?"

The chatter in the room immediately switches off while I turn several shades of red. I catch her eyes in the mirror and mouth, "Thanks a lot." She grimaces and whispers back, "Sorry."

I glance around the room and say, as breezily as possible, "That's Andy. He's the lead."

Ginger sighs. "I'll say."

Good grief. "How's your husband?" I stress the last word with as innocent a smile as I can muster.

She tugs at my hair and I catch her snarky grin in the mirror. "Jake is fine. I mean, it's football season so I never see him."

"Well, you did marry a coach."

She shrugs and the conversation lapses. I've only known Ginger since I started attending her church a few months ago and we aren't super close yet. Besides, she's married with a two-year-old boy who tears through her life like the Looney Tunes Tasmanian Devil. So I'm not entirely ready to tell her about my crush on my leading man—a crush that may or may not be reciprocated.

What is there to say? Besides, I need to save my throat as much as possible until performance time.

I remain glued to that chair long after Ginger has finished and left to find her husband and seats, where they can enjoy the show thanks to the comp tickets I gave her.

While I sit there, sucking on cough drops and zinc tablets and going over my lines in my head, I see Andy come down to the green room several times, asking the other actors to help with various tasks. He's right. He's a good delegator with natural leadership skills. Finally, thirty minutes before curtain, he stays long enough to apply makeup and finish getting into his costume.

Actually, he asks me to do his makeup. Of course I say yes. After I wash the germs off my hands with a wet wipe, I pick up the foundation. Leaning in close, I smooth a bit over his forehead and his cheeks and his bristly chin. He chews a piece of cinnamon gum and takes deep breaths. We don't talk. I'm not sure how he feels about it, but I've decided it's best not to blow my illness into his face.

Being so close feels so strange and, while applying foundation around his lips, I remember the kiss, and feel heat slide up my neck and into my face. I can't hide it. I can't leave. What can I do but hold my breath and press on? Some cheek rouge, face powder, and a bit of eyeliner and mascara, and I'm done. Except for a light, manly (or so I promise him) lip color, but I hand that over to Andy, perfectly confident he can handle it on his own.

This time, I don't blush.

He looks in the mirror as he takes care of his task. Then he steps back. "It looks good. From a distance, you can't even tell I have makeup on." He must have noticed the expression on my face because he laughs. "Yes, I know that's the whole idea. But when you don't normally wear the stuff, it can feel like you've been painted up like a clown."

I just grin.

Then he says, "I'm proud of you, Stephie. I know this is hard, especially the being quiet part."

You have no idea.

Trish comes down the stairs and shouts, "Five minutes, everyone! Five minutes!"

Andy takes my hand and pulls me to my feet. "You're going to be great."

I whisper, "So are you."

❄ ❄ ❄

And I'm right. The show comes together like peppermint and hot chocolate. The crowd loves

Andy and gives him a standing ovation. Even my cold stays out of the way. Well, for the most part.

Halfway through the play, after I exit following an intense scene, Kelvin forgets to turn off my mic right away and my coughing fit echoes across the stage and over the auditorium for a good five seconds. But, by the grace of God, I don't find out about that until the show is over.

As soon as we take our bows, I race down to the green room, slipping a bit on the cement stairs as I run, then change from costume to street clothes before the rest of the cast—who are still schmoozing the audience—can catch me *in flagrante delicto*. Since Andy has promised the cast and crew will take care of everything, all I want to do is get home and collapse onto my bed. I can't think of anything else, I'm that miserable.

It takes me less than fifteen minutes to go from theatre to apartment to bed.

I then proceed to sleep fourteen hours, waking up once for a bathroom visit and a couple of times to take an antibiotic and guzzle from a jug of water on my nightstand, trying to relieve my dry throat.

The blaring of a police siren as it streaks by my house, along with the purring of my cat right in my face, finally stir me awake. I stretch. I drink some more water and run a few vocal tests to see if I'm any better. The aches are gone. My throat still feels a bit scratchy and my sinuses are a little stuffed up. But, overall, I'm about seventy-five percent better. I pull Cozy close and say,

"So, what do you think, kitty? Can I handle another performance tonight?"

She purrs and meows and leaps to the floor, looking back at me with her, "Where's-my-lunch" face. I clear my throat. Definitely better. I flop back down on my bed, relieved, and proceed to sleep another hour … until a gnawing hunger pushes me toward the kitchen. A bowl of hot chicken noodle soup and a glass of orange juice later, and I know the worst is over.

What a relief.

Once I've taken care of Cozy, I head back to bed, this time setting my alarm for four p.m. That should give me plenty of time to shower and get to the theatre by five-fifteen.

❉ ❉ ❉

Our second performance is even better— better audience, better timing, healthier director. It just clicks. The magic of theatre, once again, thrills and surprises me. The only time I stop smiling is when it doesn't suit the scene.

In fact, it's looking to be a near-perfect performance until we're smack dab in the middle of act two. I'm standing backstage when a horrendous crash mars what was the relative quiet of a normal scene. I freeze for a second, then dash for the side curtain. An old mirror hanging on the back wall of the set has dropped, shattering into a thousand pieces, and the shock of it sends a silent panic echoing through the auditorium.

No one moves, including this fearless director who finds herself completely clueless as to what to do about this disaster. But I'm certain I don't want my actors crunching over broken glass until the next intermission. I also don't want the audience over-distracted by something that's clearly not part of the show. Like it or not, I have to fix it. Handling unexpected stage bugaboos is part of my job.

Gritting my teeth, I glance around. "Juniper, that better not be you."

Kyle, who plays Lizzie's youngest brother, Jim, is standing next to me. He must have heard me muttering because he says, "What?"

I lean toward him and whisper, "Can you get a broom and dustpan and clean up that glass?"

He stares at me, his eyes wide. "Now?"

"Well, it's as good a time as any."

With an expression that lets me know he thinks I'm crazy, Kyle shrugs and says, "Okay."

But as he walks away, I add, "Just stay in character!"

He nods and does just as I ask.

It works out even better than I imagined, actually. The other actors onstage play along, adlibbing a side joke or two and looking very much like a roomful of men who don't know what to do about a mess when a woman isn't around. The audience laughs—partly out of relief, I'm sure—and a few people even applaud the improvisation.

After the show, while I'm taking down my hair, Andy approaches me with a grin. "Was that your idea?"

"What?"

"To have the guys sweep up the glass."

"Well, yeah. I couldn't just leave it there."

"I guess not." He studies me and I would give my last cream soda to know what he's thinking. "Pretty clever."

I continue pulling bobby pins out of my hair and flinch when I yank on one a little too hard. "You don't have to seem so surprised."

"I like it when you surprise me."

Then he walks away.

Just like that.

Men.

❄ ❄ ❄

We breeze through Saturday's matinee without a hitch and barely have time to munch on chips and apples and sandwiches some friends of the theatre have brought for us before we're setting up for our final performance. I can't believe it's almost over. I savor every moment, knowing each show is a once-in-a-lifetime blessing. Sometime tomorrow afternoon, while enjoying the lifted weight of it being good and done, I will cry for thirty or forty or one-hundred-and-two minutes because it will have moved to nothing more than a happy blip on my memory meter in less than twenty-four hours.

At the beginning of act three, one of the few scenes when I'm not onstage, I have to, again, get from stage right to stage left. The best way to do that is to squeeze through a dark, narrow passageway behind a scrim and curtain at the very back of the stage. I usually try to take a small flashlight, but this time I forget. The journey requires slow, quiet steps and finesse if you don't want to trip on the many wires and cords and ropes criss-crossing the floor.

I'm halfway to the other side when a tall figure looms ahead of me. Even without his height I would have known it was Andy. Despite my slightly stuffed-up nose, I can easily discern the wonderfully clean scent of him.

We come face-to-face. I move left; he moves right. Then we both scoot the other way, a classic case of two people trying to coordinate their way around each other in the dark. Finally, Andy takes me by the shoulders and pushes me around him. We're so close, his body brushes against mine. I glance up and catch the glint of his eyes in the dark.

Then his hands tighten and he pulls me up and kisses me. This one is even more sudden … and so much longer. He tilts his head and deepens the kiss as I wrap my arms around his neck. I can barely breathe through my still-damaged sinuses, but I don't care. Emotions rattle through me like an old locomotive. I'm not sure how long it lasts, but it's long enough for my fingers to explore every bump and curve on the top of his head.

Finally, the realization that we have a scene coming up brings me to my senses, and I push him away. I gulp down pillows of air to still my racing heart. I can't very well go onstage flushed and wheezing.

Andy's hands slide all the way down my arms. A simple yet intoxicating caress. He squeezes my fingers and whispers, "Thanks."

With that, he turns and slips away, while I stare at his retreating back, dumbfounded.

Thanks? What in the name of Ding Dongs is he thanking me for? But I don't have time to wonder because, in the next instant, I hear my cue and realize I'm late. Sending a quick prayer that the other actors will cover for me, I hurry to the wing, stage left, from where I make my entrance.

And proceed to perform the scene with the sweaty awkwardness of a chubby kid in gym shorts, slowly stewing at kiss-'em-and-thank-'em Andy the whole time.

❄ ❄ ❄

And, just like that, we're done. I haven't talked to Andy since the behind-the-curtain incident, not sure what to say. I still don't have a clue what he's thinking, so I suppose there's nothing to do but wait it out. Chances are good we'll say good-bye after the cast party and I won't see him again until next spring ... *if* he auditions for the summer musical.

But before we can celebrate our success with pizza and fun moments and stories about all the things that could have gone wrong but, miraculously, didn't, we need to strike the set.

Men and women, including several who've volunteered to stay after the show and help, crowd the stage, pulling out nails and stacking scenery flats. My main job is to tell people who the various items belong to or show them where theatre-owned pieces need to go.

While going through the props with Trish, I see a well-dressed businessman greet Andy with a handshake. A platinum-blonde Jean Harlow wannabe, draped in red chiffon and white cashmere with ruby and gold jewelry cascading from her ears and throat, stands at the businessman's side, sliding her hand down Andy's arm and sizing him up like he's a French silk pie.

I don't like her.

When Andy glances my way and frowns, I like her even less. Our eyes meet, briefly, before he turns away. I huff a breath into my bangs, which don't budge thanks to layers of gel and hairspray. I'm sure I look lovely, with my dripping, stage-makeup raccoon eyes, after-performance jeans and T-shirt, and worked-over theatre hair. Right. I know without even glancing in the mirror that I'm wilting. Jean Harlow, on the other hand, seems more than ready for her close-up.

Yet even though I realize it will be like a sick duck approaching an elegant swan, I can't help myself. Until Andy tells me otherwise, I choose to believe there's a chance for us. I sneeze three times on the way over, which I'm sure does wonderful things for my nose and eyes, but I don't care. If Andy prefers someone like her then he doesn't want someone like me.

Still, I strut over there like I just stepped out of a fashion magazine. Let them scoff at my—

And I trip over a bump in the floor, catching myself before I sprawl across the stage by doing a sloppy two-step with a skip and a jump. Then I grin, sneeze once more, and say,

"Did you get all your costume pieces from the green room yet, Andy?"

Brilliant, Stephie. The blonde smirks at me with all the confidence of a woman who has never had a rival in her life. But then I notice the smile on Andy's face.

Unless I'm completely mistaken—always a possibility—he might actually like me. His eyes dart to my lips for a tap of a second, and heat crawls up my neck. Jean Harlow's face tightens slightly as she glances between us.

Let her wonder.

"Not yet," Andy says, then frowns again, clears his throat, and indicates the businessman. "Stephie Graham, this is Pat Hansen. We, uh, work together. And his date, Jessica Withers."

Jessica. Joan. Jean. Whatever. I shake their hands. Their cold, better-than-me hands.

Hansen laughs. "Don't be so modest, Andrew." Then Mr. Business slaps a hand on Andy's back and turns to me. "This young man is going to help me buy this place."

"Buy this place?" I look at Andy. "Are you kidding me?"

His spreads his hands wide, trying to look innocent. "Stephie, it's just—"

"I couldn't be less interested in your excuses." Surprise fills his eyes and I add, "Apparently, you're an even better actor than I thought."

He grabs my arm but I jerk away and race toward the backstage area. Without giving it much thought, I take the stairs toward the green room at a run, realizing too late I'll be trapped down there if Andy comes after me.

As if he would.

But my foot hits the top step on a skid before I have time to change my mind and the next thing I know I'm flying, horizontal, and heading straight toward the unforgiving cement floor below.

Chapter 10
Juniper

She stood behind the curtain, stage right, biting her lip as she waited for Mr. Van Meer to invite her onstage to take her bows ... and to accept the large bouquet of red roses he held in his arms. But the distinguished gentleman was feeling especially verbose this night. Juniper wasn't sure what he was talking about, but she did know he'd mentioned "during this festive season" at least a handful of times.

Not that she minded. In fact, she appreciated the time to decide what she should say to the audience. It was one thing to sing in front of hundreds of people; it was quite another to stand before them and try to find her own words—the right words—to express how she felt.

The next moment, though, Mr. Van Meer swung his arm her way and called her name and decision time was ended. So she smiled as she swept onto the stage, surprised and humbled to see the crowd surge to their feet once more. Mr. Van Meer handed her the bouquet. She thanked him, then turned to the audience.

The stage lights blared into her eyes, blinding her until they dimmed and the house lights came up. She smiled at the faces she recognized—her mother and father, several women from the Ladies' Aid Society, the Wellesleys.

And William. Her heart studded against her ribs. He stood in the front row, clapping, his face passive and proud. Juniper gulped down her shock, and curtsied, to him more than anyone else. She smiled, murmured a thank you, then froze as a stunning woman with jet black hair looped her hand around Will's arm. The ring on her left hand shimmered in the light.

Juniper felt the color drain from her face. She took one final bow and hurried to the relative sanctuary behind the heavy stage curtain. Her heart trembled.

Could it be possible? Had he really found someone else so quickly? Someone ... permanent? Vaguely aware of the audience milling around the auditorium and the prick of rose thorns in her arms, Juniper wondered if she'd ever felt so lost.

He didn't want her. It was over. The words "spinster" and "brokenhearted" thudded through her brain.

"Juniper! Juniper, look who's here!"

Her mother. Her sweet, clueless mother. Now what?

I have to get away. The light to the basement dressing room beckoned to her, and she started for the stairs. But a movement toward the stage grabbed her attention. Peter Billings stood near the curtain, caught in the glow of what few lights still lit the theatre. He wore a new, blue, double-breasted suit and he looked handsome, grown-up.

Determined. Even with the flop of hair across his forehead, something was different. Juniper glanced back at the stairs, wondering if she should run *away* from whatever beckoned to her in his eyes ... or *to* it.

Her mother's words from September come back to her:

You're only a victim if you make yourself one.

Peter took a step closer. She whispered the name her heart ached for.

It wasn't *William.* The thought frightened her more than she had ever expected. She turned ... and rushed for the stairs.

Chapter 11
Stephie

I stand at the bottom of the stairs, stunned. What just happened? Did I fall? I was falling; I'm sure of it. The next thing I knew I ... wasn't. Andy yells my name and I glance up.

He hurries toward me. "Are you okay?"

"Uh, yeah. Why wouldn't I be?"

"You screamed."

"I did?"

"Yeah." He studies me, head to foot and back. "A blood-curdling scream. Like someone just stabbed you in the stomach."

"Oh. I don't remember that."

I glance around. Seriously, what just happened? "I slipped on the stairs and fell. Or I didn't. I don't know."

"You seem fine."

"I feel fine."

"Though, you *are* trembling."

He's right. My hands are shaking more than they do when I drink too much caffeine.

Andy smiles and shakes his head. "I guess you have an angel watching over you."

Do I really? I've always felt so alone. It would be nice to have real, physical evidence that I'm not. Except I don't have physical evidence. Just a weird case of a few seconds of my life that have disappeared without explanation. Seconds that might mean everything.

Or nothing. Except, perhaps, I'm losing my mind.

And yet ... something on Andy's face tells me I'm going to be just fine. He grins again, looking all hopeful and cute, like the hero in a Hallmark Christmas movie. And I want him to kiss me already, until I remember he plans to cash in on my theatre.

So, instead of putting my hand on his and smiling back, I say, "Why would you do this?"

The smile fades. "It's not what you think, Stephie."

"It's not? Because it would seem you want to make money on seeing the Holland turned into a parking lot. Or a Dollar General."

He grabs me by the shoulders and—I'm not kidding—shakes me like a broken gumball dispenser. "Honey, you have got to stop jumping to conclusions or you're gonna hurt yourself."

There he goes again, trying to make me fall in love with him. Forget tumbling down a flight of stairs; this is a fall I might never recover from. So I back away. "Explain then. You don't have to rattle my teeth loose."

"Yes, Hansen and a group of investors want to buy the Holland ..." He holds up a hand to halt my interruption. "But not to tear it down. They want to restore it. Bring it back to its original glory."

Oh, poo. "Really?"

"I swear. I love this old theatre. I want to be in more shows." Then he flicks his eyebrows at me. "But only if you're the director, of course."

Now I can smile. "Of course."

❊ ❊ ❊

Two hours later, with the set cleared, the pizza gone, and most of the cast and crew having hugged their good-byes before heading home, Merle and I still sit slouched in theatre seats, sipping on sodas and talking about what went right and what we need to do different next time.

"Overall," he says, "it was a fair success."

"I agree."

"And you were an excellent Lizzie."

Sweet man. "Thanks, Merle."

I glance around the darkened theatre. "Other than the mirror, we didn't have any serious problems during the performances. Maybe Juniper approved after all."

"Maybe."

"Shoot. I still haven't had a chance to talk to Cora. Hopefully, I can visit her next week."

"Coraletta Jones?"

"Yeah." Why does he sound so confused? "You said she could tell me about Juniper."

"Oh, right." He rakes a hand over his hair, his eyes apologetic. "Well, not anymore. She had a stroke last week. Coraletta's not talking to anyone. Besides, she's in her nineties. I'm not sure how much she'd remember anyway."

Too late. Sadness for Coraletta and sadness because of the story she can't tell me now makes me want to cry. I don't, but I want to. "I'm so sorry to hear that."

"I'm sorry too, Stephanie."

"Even just knowing what Juniper looked like would be nice."

He shifts in his seat. "Oh, well, there's a picture of her in the back." Merle stands, a little more slowly than usual. "Come on, then. I'll show you."

Andy appears out of the backstage area. I hadn't realized he was still around and, for a moment, wonder what he's been up to. I say, "Merle's going to show me a photo of Juniper if you're interested."

His eyes widen, sending twinkling green sparks my way. "Try and stop me."

We follow Merle to a tall, old filing cabinet in the back. After rustling through a few drawers, he finally pulls out a framed photo and hands it to me.

Of course it's old and in black and white but the picture shows two rows of women; some smiling, some not. Merle points to the saddest one in the group.

She's beautiful, with deep, wide eyes and smooth hair that sweeps across her forehead in a thick wave. Her dress is sleek and satin and she has on white, elbow-length gloves. Her hands are folded serenely in front of her.

Andy says, "She's pretty, but she's not happy."

Merle nods and clears his throat. "Well, I'm beat. Can you two lock up if I head home?"

"Sure we can." I put a hand on his arm. "Thanks for all your help, Merle."

"Any time."

He shuffles away. Andy and I just stand there, brooding. Well, I am, anyway. Poor, sad Juniper. Would my story have an ending just as depressing? I glance up at the man next to me. No reason to think it won't.

"Thanks for staying," I say as we switch off the lights.

"Sure."

Various other topics scroll through my brain and I finally land on one. "What are your Thanksgiving plans?"

"Oh, you know. Family stuff."

The only brilliant thing I can think to say to that is, "Oh, nice."

We head back to the auditorium, and I load up my arms with bags of costumes and scripts and whatever else I need to take home. Without my having to say anything, Andy picks up the empty pizza boxes and a large garbage bag stuffed with trash and follows me out the side entrance.

"So," he says, "how will you spend the holiday?"

"A family from church invited me over."

"That's cool."

"Yeah, it's nice. I have a standing invitation with them for any holiday when I don't have somewhere to go."

He drops the garbage in a dumpster. "Is it hard?"

"What?"

"Not having a family."

"Well, no. I mean, it's just the way it is." Not that I haven't fantasized as to what it would be like to be part of a family. But dreams are cheap and only hurt for a moment. Then I move on.

I always move on.

He says, "I really enjoyed working with you, Stephie."

I smile. The end is near. "Me too. I hope you'll participate in future productions. The summer musical is always a lot of fun."

"Yeah, I'm planning on it."

He walks me to my car, slow, hesitant. "So, I'll call you. We'll get together."

"That sounds great."

He just stands there for a month of moments, staring at me, and I wonder what he's mulling over. But whatever he wanted to say comes out as, "Well, I'll see ya."

Then I watch him mosey out of my life, much like he moseyed into it two months before.

He doesn't call.

❄ ❄ ❄

A month later, I shuffle around my cold apartment, setting a different kind of stage. A Christmas-y one.

To save money, I've put the thermostat at a crisp sixty-four degrees, and compensate for the chill by layering on an aqua turtleneck, a cream sweater, and a deep blue-and-cream-striped hoodie, completing the look by draping a purple Sherpa throw across my shoulders. The calendar declares it's Christmas Eve, and I've decided to celebrate by roasting a small turkey breast with all the trimmings. I'll have enough leftovers to last me until the New Year.

I turn on the twinkle lights on my plastic, three-foot Christmas tree as well as the strands draped around the room and across the useless but homey white-brick fireplace.

Happiness is all about the mood lighting.

After firing up an evergreen-scented candle, because that's part of my happy place too, and sticking my copy of *Chitty Chitty Bang Bang* in the DVD player, I settle on the couch with Cozy on my lap. Not having a family of my own, I've created my own traditions, and a little Dick Van Dyke zipping around in a flying car is a big part of that.

Right in the middle of "Toot Sweets," the doorbell rings. My heart jumps because no one ever comes to visit. And who would show up after five p.m. on Christmas Eve?

I pause the movie, then tiptoe over to the door. Peering through the peephole, I almost drop to the floor. But I don't. Instead, I glance in the coat rack mirror to make sure I look presentable, and quietly thank God for nudging me to take a shower earlier. No makeup but clean hair. I open the door.

Andy stands there, smiling, with his hands behind his back. "Hey. Merry Christmas."

"Merry Christmas." He looks great. Cold and scruffy and huggable. In two seconds I've managed to push the fact that I haven't heard from him for over a month to the back of my brain, I'm that happy to see him.

So I step aside and swing my hand to indicate the living room. "Come on in."

And he does. He glances around, taking in my sparse but snug furnishings and the strings of Christmas lights. "Smells good in here."

"Thanks. I'm making a turkey."

He steps back, suddenly flustered. "Oh, sorry. I didn't know you were expecting company."

"I'm not. Can't a single gal make a Christmas bird?"

"Sure." He grins again. Then we just stand there, happy to be together. Well, I am, anyway. And he certainly seems happy.

"So," Andy says, "I was doing a little research on the Holland and found something I thought might interest you." He hands me a piece of paper.

It's a copy of a *Bellefontaine Examiner* article from September 1948. The headline reads "Local Singing Star Returns Home for Benefit." And there's a picture of a beautiful woman with the name "Juniper Remington-Billings" printed underneath.

I murmur, "You found her."

"Yes, I did."

I glance up, smiling. "I guess she didn't die."

"Nope. Well, eventually, but not until years later, when she was in her eighties, according to the records I found."

"Which means the Holland doesn't have a ghost. At least, not a brokenhearted one." Though I never really believed the theatre was haunted, I'm still a little surprised by my disappointment. I hold up the article. "Where did you get this?"

"It took a little digging." He tilts his head, his eyes blazing into mine. "But it was worth it."

Oh. "You did this for me?" I seem to be having trouble speaking louder than a whisper.

He takes my hand. The Sherpa throw slides to the floor. "I missed you, Stephie. I'm sorry I didn't call."

"It's a busy time of year." Not that I consider that an excuse but I'm just so glad to see him I really don't care. "Still, why did you come by tonight? On Christmas Eve?"

"Oh, well, long story." He points to the couch and I nod. He takes a seat; I pick up Cozy and drop down next to him. "I was at my sister's, eating caramel corn and watching the kids beg to open presents and—" He glances toward the TV. "Is that *Chitty Chitty Bang Bang?*"

I follow his gaze. I'd paused the DVD right in the middle of an impressive kick line by the dancers. "Um, yeah."

"Love that movie."

"You do?"

"I always wanted to be an inventor like Caractacus Potts when I was a kid."

Cute. He stares at the screen for a second and I come this close to asking if he wants to watch the movie with me. Instead I say,

"Andy, why are you here?"

"Oh, right." He takes a deep breath, facing me again. "Brenda made me come over."

Well, that's flattering. "She did? Why?"

He scrunches up his nose and scratches his chin. "Her exact words were, 'Stop moping around and go get your woman.'"

"She said that?"

"Yep."

I remind myself to breathe and whisper, "Is it true?"

He puts his hand along the side of my face, brushing my hair back by drawing a line from my forehead to my neck with his fingertips. "Yes." Then his lips follow the same line his fingers had.

And now I might never breathe normally again.

"I really like you, Stephie. If how much I've missed you this last month is any indication, it's a bit more than 'like.'" He leans back, and I miss his warmth. Then he says,

"I want you to come home with me."

Home.

I say, "Okay," and hear a bell ding, like I just answered a question right on a quiz show. I pull back, confused. Then,

"Oh, the turkey's done."

He laughs and I laugh. Something needs to be done about it, but I'm fuzzy as to what that might be.

Then he says, "Well, are you going to get it?"

"Get it? Oh, right." Skipping into the kitchen, I pull out the turkey. It looks good—golden and juicy. Definitely edible. If the man of my dreams wasn't sitting on my couch, I'd be nibbling on it already. Instead, I set it on the counter and turn off the oven, then skitter back to Andy and plop down next to him. I say,

"So, you really do like me."

"Yeah, I guess I do."

I shake my head. "Why?" Because it can't possibly be true.

"Why?" He looks at the ceiling, like he has to think about it. I almost hit him. He chuckles and says, "Maybe it's because you're so clever." And he kisses my forehead.

"Well, I can't deny that."

"Or it's your sense of humor." This kiss lands on my nose. "Or because you're so talented." His lips slide across my cheek. "And sweet."

Okay, that's enough of that. I put both hands on either side of his face and kiss him. But only for a second, because he pulls away.

"Wait a minute … why do you like me?"

I shrug. "Honestly, I wouldn't know where to start."

"Well, at least try."

"All right." I tilt my head, just like he always does. "You're very nice-looking. And strong. And you have good teeth."

He rolls his eyes. "I'm not a horse, Stephie."

I giggle. "Fair enough. I guess … it's mostly … I mean the main reason—"

"Spit it out, hon."

"Fine. You make me feel … safe." Then, praying it isn't too soon, I add, "Like I'm part of something."

"Something?"

"Yes."

"Like a family?"

Biting my thumbnail, I give my attention to everything but him. "Maybe."

"It's okay."

I look into his eyes. Those warm, Christmas-green eyes. "Really? It's not too weird?"

He smiles. "If that's weird, we're all weird."

So I grab him by his wonderfully bald head once again and make out with my weird, mosey-through-life, realtor boyfriend. Until he pushes me away and clears his throat and invites me to his sister's for Christmas dinner. Because, well, that's just the kind of man he is.

❄ ❄ ❄

That night, I dream about Juniper. She looks like she did in the picture I saw at the Holland Theatre—young and beautiful and sad. Then, like a spark landing on dry twigs, she alights with a smile and skips away, daring me to follow. She leads me to a sun-draped field where flowers droop in the browns and tears of fall. A boy waits for her there—cute but strong with shaggy hair and grown-up eyes. Juniper jumps into his arms;

they laugh and kiss and fade into the trees and sky. Then I wake up.

My mouth and throat are desert-dry but waves of happy endings wash over me. Maybe Juniper's life wasn't so sad.

Maybe we both have a story to tell.

Early-morning sunlight glistens off snow-covered trees and filters through my curtains, calling me to the day. I slide out of bed, smiling.

Today, for the first time in years, I won't spend Christmas on my own but with Andy and his family.

Maybe, someday soon, *my* family.

I need to get ready.

The End

Theatre Terms

Acts – a division of a script, usually made up of *scenes*. Intermissions are often taken between acts.

Blocking – stage movements and positions worked out by the director so actors know where they have to be without bumping into each other.

Cold Read – reading aloud/performing a script without prior preparation, usually for an audition.

Cues – a prearranged line or action that indicates to actors, crew members, or stage technicians what the next line or action is.

Flat – a *flat* piece of scenery usually consisting of a wooden frame covered with stretched fabric or lauan, a thin plywood with a smooth surface that's easy to paint.

Read-through – a first rehearsal of a play during which the actors read their lines from scripts.

Scenes – shorter sections that make up the play's *acts*.

Scrim – a plain or painted gauzy curtain that can be opaque or translucent, depending on the lighting.

Sides – a few pages containing a specific set of lines handed out at an audition.

Strike the Set – the process of disassembling a set once a production has ended.

Tech Week – the last week of rehearsals before a performance during which all of the technical elements are present for the first time.

Wings – the backstage areas on each side of the stage, which the audience typically can't see.